# Reading Together

Before you start reading, it helps to talk about what you think might happen in the story.

**Have you seen these characters before? What are they like? What will happen to them in the story? Why do you think that? Does the title help you? Are there any clues on the cover?**

Sound out unfamiliar words and look for clues in the pictures. Sometimes the words before and after an unknown word can help you work out what a difficult word means.

After you've finished the story, go back to any words that you found tricky and talk about what they mean.

# Activities for After Reading

Can you spot these challenging words in this story?

**tame**   **passive**   **potions**   **fluttered**   **tropical**

**aquarium**   **inventory**   **shuffled**   **quest**

What does each word mean? How do you know? Can you put the word into a sentence? Talk about what you think will happen in Emmy, Birch, Byte and Ink's next adventure.

# Question Time!

What are Emmy and Birch looking for? What problems do they have when looking? Do they succeed?

# Advanced Question

Do you think Emmy made a good choice? Why do you think that? Would you have chosen differently?

Birch threw a stick
high into the air.
It flew above the houses
of a Minecraft village.

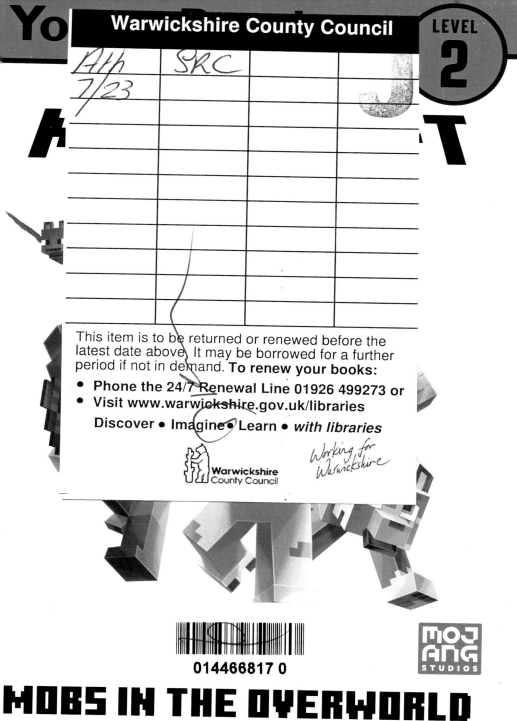

014466817 0

**MOJANG STUDIOS**

# MOBS IN THE OVERWORLD

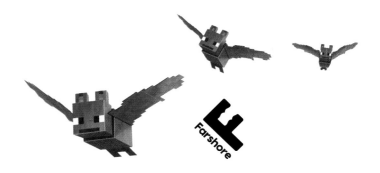

First published in the United States by Random House Children's Books
and in Canada by Penguin Random House Canada Limited.

First published in Great Britain in 2021 by Farshore
An imprint of HarperCollins*Publishers*
1 London Bridge Street, London SE1 9GF
www.farshore.co.uk

HarperCollins*Publishers*
Macken House, 39/40 Mayor Street Upper,
Dublin 1, D01 C9W8, Ireland

Written by Nick Eliopulos
Illustrated by Alan Batson

ISBN 978 0 7555 0044 4
Printed in the United Kingdom
006

MIX
Paper | Supporting
responsible forestry
FSC™ C007454

This book is produced from independently certified FSC™ paper
to ensure responsible forest management.

For more information visit: www.harpercollins.co.uk/green

His pet wolf, Byte,
ran after the stick.
His friend Emmy did not
have a pet.
But she had a plan
to find one.

"Let's go exploring,"
said Emmy. "Somewhere
in the Overworld,
I will find my perfect pet."
Birch cheered.
Byte wagged his tail.
They liked exploring.

The creatures of Minecraft
were called mobs.
Emmy and Birch knew
that some mobs were peaceful
and some mobs were hostile.

There were many passive mobs
in the village. Emmy saw sheep
and chickens, a pig and a cow.
"These mobs belong to the
villagers," Birch said.
Emmy agreed, so they
went looking elsewhere
for a mob to tame.

In a chilly forest called a taiga,
they found three rabbits.
Emmy thought they were very cute.
But she did not want to take a
bunny from its family.
Byte scared a fox away. GRRRR!

Birch spotted a bees' nest.

What luck!

Emmy could keep the bees,

and he could collect the honey.

"Wait!" cried Emmy.

Birch only wanted to knock
the nest out of the tree,
but he had forgotten
to build a campfire. Now the bees
were angry. BUZZZZZZ!

The bees chased Emmy,
Birch and Byte
out of the woods.

"Bugs do not make good pets,"
said Emmy. "No bees, please.
And no spiders."

"And no silverfish!"
said Birch. "Yuck!"

13

The friends entered a cave.
It was a shortcut
through the mountain.
They saw some bats
sleeping high above.
But there were other mobs
living in the dark – hostile mobs!

Emmy and Birch saw movement
in the shadows.

A slime bounced.

A skeleton rode towards them
on a spider's back.

A zombie shuffled.

Byte leapt at the skeleton,
while Birch fought the spider.
Emmy used her bow
to send arrows flying
at the zombie and
the slime.

All the noise woke the bats!
They fluttered everywhere!
There was a light ahead.
Emmy and Birch fought
their way towards it.

They made it! Phew!
Outside the cavern,
the sun was still shining.
The friends soon found a
jungle full of bamboo,
where a baby panda
was doing flips in the grass.

18

ACHOO!

The baby panda sneezed.

A slimeball flew

from the panda's nose

and almost hit Birch!

Maybe a panda was not

Emmy's perfect pet.

19

They looked in the ocean.
Emmy swam with a dolphin,
while Birch fought
a drowned.

They saw tropical fish, a squid
and a school of pufferfish.
Emmy did not have
an aquarium.
There were no pets for her here.

21

Next, they explored the snow and ice.
While Birch and Byte
fought with a frozen skeleton
called a stray,
Emmy searched for a pet.

She saw a polar bear cub
that was adorable –
but the mama bear growled
when Emmy got too close! GRRRR!
Emmy decided that a polar bear cub
would not want to be tamed.

Finally, after much exploring,
they came to a swamp.
Byte barked loudly
and pointed with his nose.

"It's a cat!" said Birch.
"Follow it," said Emmy.

But the black cat
belonged to a wicked witch.
She giggled and threw colourful potions.
Emmy, Birch and Byte
ran away as fast as they could.
Some potions could be harmful.

They ran all the way
out of the swamp.
They did not hear
the HISS of a creeper
until it was too late!

The hostile mob exploded!

The explosion left a hole
in the ground, but Emmy,
Birch and Byte were all okay.
Emmy was worried.
"What if I never find a pet?"
Birch told Emmy that
she should not give up,
and Byte licked her cheek.

Suddenly, they realised
there was a horse nearby,
standing in the grass of the plains.
It was the most beautiful mob
Emmy had ever seen.

Birch crafted a lead.

He made it with string

from a spider and the slimeball

from the baby panda sneeze.

Emmy walked towards the horse.

Her movements were slow and quiet.

Emmy took the lead from Birch
while he gave the horse an apple.
"I will name her Ink," said Emmy.
Birch pulled a saddle out of his inventory.
"You'll need this."
Emmy saddled Ink and climbed on.

Emmy galloped home on Ink's back.
Birch and Byte ran alongside them.
Their quest into the world of mobs
to find a pet had been a success.